THE Berenstain BEAR SCOUTS

and the
Sci-Fi Pizza

Look for more books in
The Berenstain Bear Scouts series:

*The Berenstain Bear Scouts
in Giant Bat Cave*

*The Berenstain Bear Scouts
and the Humongous Pumpkin*

*The Berenstain Bear Scouts
Meet Bigpaw*

*The Berenstain Bear Scouts
Save That Backscratcher*

*The Berenstain Bear Scouts
and the Terrible Talking Termite*

*The Berenstain Bear Scouts
and the Coughing Catfish*

THE Berenstain BEAR SCOUTS

and the
Sci-Fi Pizza

by Stan & Jan Berenstain
Illustrated by Michael Berenstain

A
LITTLE APPLE
PAPERBACK

SCHOLASTIC INC.
New York Toronto London Auckland Sydney

ISBN 0-590-60385-X

12 11 10 9 8 7 6 5 4 3   7 8 9/9 0 1/0

Printed in the U.S.A.   40

First Scholastic printing, October 1996

• Table of Contents •

1. The Order of the Day   1
2. In Farmer Ben's Far Meadow   7
3. First Things First   14
4. Spooky Ground   17
5. The New Ralph   21
6. Gotcha!   27
7. Help from the Professor   33
8. All the Pizza You Can Eat *Forever*!   36
9. A Knife in the Door!   39
10. Flight Test   42
11. Down a Weasel Hole   49
12. Waiting for Ralph   55
13. In the Dough   58
14. Pizza Party   63
15. "You Should Have Seen It, Gramps!"   67
16. A Daring Plan   71
17. Tops in Toppings   74
18. "Ready! Get Set! *Twirl!*"   79
19. The Battle of the Joysticks   86
20. Follow That Pizza!   91

THE Berenstain BEAR SCOUTS
and the
Sci-Fi Pizza

• Chapter 1 •

The Order of the Day

There's no doubt that if Bear Scouts Brother, Sister, Fred, and Lizzy had known that the weasels had targeted them for revenge they would have been worried — especially since the targeter was Weasel McGreed himself. McGreed was the leader of the weasel gang that lived in Weaselworld, a secret underground network of tunnels, caves, offices, workshops, and laboratories.

McGreed's underground empire had everything he would need to reach his sworn goal: to steal Bear Country from

tho boaro, to tako it ovor look, otook, and
honeypot.

Not that McGreed thought it would be
an easy task. The weasels were tough and
wiry. But McGreed knew they were no
match for the big, powerful bears. Why,
even a bear cub could toss a weasel
around as if it were a beanbag.

But the weasels were not about to give
up on their goal of taking over Bear Country. Even though they were no match for
the bears in size, they had two things
working for them: super smarts and super
secrecy. But something had just happened
that made McGreed think that Weaselworld's secrecy had broken down. He was
very angry about it.

Three of McGreed's most important
weasels were walking along one of the
many torch-lit tunnels of Weaselworld.
They were on their way to see the archweasel. They weren't very happy about it.

The group included General Maxx,
commander of the weasel armies, Dr.
Boffins, Weaselworld's chief scientist, and
Stye, a tunnel tough who had come up the
hard way and was McGreed's chief lieu-
tenant. Even though they were VIWs (Very
Important Weasels), they looked like school
cubs who had been called to the princi-
pal's office. You could hardly blame them.
McGreed had a terrible temper. Even his
whisper was frightening. And he could go
from a whisper to a foaming-at-the-mouth
screaming rage in the wink of an eye.

The door guards came to attention and
saluted as the VIWs neared McGreed's of-

fice. As soon as they entered the office they knew they were in trouble. They could tell from McGreed's body language. It said BIG TROUBLE. He was seated at the end of a long table. As he sat drumming his fingers on the table, his little yellow eyes glared at them through the gloom. There was a film projector beside him. He reached out and punched a button. A beam of light stabbed the darkness and projected a picture on a giant screen. A shocking picture.

It was a picture of Bear Scouts Brother, Sister, Fred, and Lizzy. When General Maxx saw it his heart sank. He knew right away that the picture had been taken by one of Weaselworld's security cameras. He could tell from the picture's torch-lit tunnel background. Somehow the Bear Scouts had broken the secrecy of Weaselworld. There was no question about it. The picture was proof.

General Maxx was in charge of security. So he expected a big bawling out. He wasn't disappointed. Words like "fool," "idiot," and "traitor" bounced off the walls of McGreed's cavelike office. McGreed was in a fury. "It's your job to protect Weaselworld from prying eyes!" he roared. "And what do you do? You allow those disgusting Bear Scouts to walk around Weaselworld as if they owned it! Those same scouts who foiled my beautiful humongous pumpkin scheme. Do you remember that, my dear general?"

How could Maxx forget? The pumpkin scheme had cost him his general's stars. He'd never be able to look a pumpkin in the face again. It had taken him a long time to work his way back up to general.

McGreed, who had gone from finger-drumming to a towering rage, had gone back to finger-drumming.

"Stye," said McGreed.

"Yes, Archweasel," said Stye.

"Take down the order of the day," said McGreed.

Quickly, Stye had pencil and paper ready.

"The order of the day," said McGreed, "is *the death and destruction of the Bear Scouts!*

"*Corporal* Maxx," said McGreed, "you are dismissed."

The former general slunk out of the room.

"Stye," said McGreed. "You and Dr. Boffins stay. We need to talk."

• Chapter 2 •

In Farmer Ben's Far Meadow

As fate would have it, Scouts Brother, Sister, Fred, and Lizzy were crossing a field directly above the archweasel's office. They were just about to climb through the fence into Farmer Ben's far meadow.

"Last one through the fence is a squashed frog," shouted Fred.

"No fair!" said Brother. He had reason to complain. He was carrying a large red and yellow model airplane and was the last one to get through.

"I guess you're the squashed frog," said

Fred. He and Sister were laughing. But not Lizzy.

"I wish you wouldn't say things like that," said Lizzy.

"Things like what?" said Fred.

"Last one through the fence is a squashed frog," said Lizzy.

"It's just an expression," said Fred.

"That may be," said Lizzy. "But it's not very respectful of frogs."

"Gee," said Fred. "You can't say anything around here anymore."

"That's our Lizzy," said Sister with a grin. Sister gave Lizzy, who was her best friend as well as her fellow scout, a little hug. "Don't worry, Liz," she said. "If he says it again I'll pop him."

That's the way it was with Lizzy. She loved animals. And not just cuddly big-eyed animals. She had just as big a hello for worms, spiders, and beetles.

The "one for all and all for one!" scouts

were a strong team. They not only got along together, they worked well together. But each member of the troop was also his or her own person with special talents and interests. Lizzy had her way with animals. While Sister was no fool, she did tend to rush in where angels feared to tread. It wouldn't be fair to say that Fred, who read the dictionary and the encyclopedia just for fun, was a nerd. But it wouldn't be exactly unfair either.

Brother, who was the unofficial troop leader (the *official* troop leader was Scout Leader Jane), was an all-around sort of a cub. He was good at sports and had lots of hobbies. His favorite hobby was building and flying model airplanes. That's why they were in Farmer Ben's far meadow: to fly Brother's first gasoline-powered model plane. Until now he had built and flown only rubber-band–powered planes.

"What are you doing with that eyedropper?" said Sister.

"Gassing up the engine," said Brother.

"Why with an eyedropper?" said Lizzy.

"Look," said Brother. "I spent weeks building this thing. And I saved up for months to buy the engine. If I put in too much gas, it could just fly away. Fred, hold on to the tail while I turn the engine over. But don't let 'er go until I say so."

Brother turned the propeller the way they do with old-fashioned planes in black and white movies. After a couple of turns

the little engine came to life with a snarl.
What a racket! The reason they were over
here in Farmer Ben's far meadow was the
noise.

"Okay! Let 'er go!" shouted Brother.

The plane snarled up into the air as if
it were after something.

"Wow! Look at 'er go!" cried Sister.

"Wowee!" cried Lizzy. She watched the plane and ran after it as it climbed higher and higher. But as so often happens when you aren't looking where you're going, Lizzy took a tumble. Luckily, it was a soft grassy field, so she didn't get hurt. But the fall did take her breath away. She sat in the grass and watched the plane. The rest of the troop came a-running.

"Are you hurt?" said Sister.

"I'm fine," said Lizzy. "But look! There's another plane up there. And they're going to crash into each other!"

The scouts looked up. Sure enough, there *was* another plane up there. But they weren't going to crash.

"Relax," said Fred. "That's a real airplane. It's at least two thousand feet higher than the model."

The real airplane was a biplane. The

kind that pulls advertising signs. It was pulling one.

"What's it say?" said Sister, trying to read it. That's when the plane's snarl turned into a series of burps.

"What's wrong?" said Lizzy.

"Nothing," said Brother. "It's just running out of gas, that's all."

The plane headed down.

"That's funny," said Sister. "When I run out of gas is when I *stop* burping."

"Very funny," said Brother. "Come on. Let's get the plane."

" 'Calling all bears!' " said Lizzy. " 'Pizza Shack is coming to Beartown! See our ad in today's paper!' "

"Huh?" said Fred.

"That's what it says on the sign that plane's pulling."

The rest of the troop stopped and looked up.

"So it does," said Fred.

• Chapter 3 •

First Things First

McGreed and Stye watched as Dr. Boffins paced back and forth in front of the arch-weasel's desk. "Hmm," he said. "You want me to design a foolproof security system that will protect Weaselworld from prying eyes."

"A *Bear Scout*–proof security system," said McGreed.

"And you want it as soon as possible," said Dr. Boffins, still pacing.

"I want it *yesterday*!" cried McGreed, pounding on his desk.

"Hmm," said Dr. Boffins, still pacing. "A

Bear Scout–proof security system yesterday. Now, let me see. It would have to combine an alarm system with a capture system. Uh-huh. Yes. Yes. That might work. On the other hand, it might be better to reverse the process and combine a capture system with an alarm system . . ."

It didn't take much to irritate the archweasel. He was beginning to get very irritated watching Dr. Boffins pace back and forth, back and forth. But McGreed kept his temper. Dr. Boffins was a scientific genius. It was he who had invented the magic pumpkin seed that grew into the humongous pumpkin. It wasn't his fault that the scheme had failed. It was those

HMMM · · ·

sneaking, snooping, good-for-nothing Bear
Scouts. Just the thought of them made his
neck fur stand on end.

Finally, McGreed couldn't hold his temper any longer. "Well, Boffins! Can you do
it?" he screamed.

"Huh? Wha?" said Boffins. "I beg your
pardon, sir?"

"I said," said McGreed, "do you think
you can make such a security system?"

"Why, yes. Of course I can, sir," said
Boffins.

"Stye," said McGreed. "Would you take
the good doctor back to his laboratory so
he can start work?"

"This way, doctor," said Stye, taking
Boffins by the arm. As he was about to
leave, he turned. "Chief," he said. "About
that order of the day . . ."

"First things first," said McGreed.
"First the security system. *Then* the death
and destruction."

• Chapter 4 •

Spooky Ground

"How about that," said Sister. "Pizza Shack is coming to Beartown."

Sister, Lizzy, and Fred were strolling toward the far end of the field, where Brother's out-of-gas plane had landed. He had run ahead to check things out.

"I went to one once when I was in Big Bear City with my dad," said Fred.

"How was it?" said Lizzy.

"Super!" said Fred. "They had crusty pizza, deep-dish pizza, and every kind of pizza in between. They had more kinds of toppings than Bearskin and Robbins has ice cream flavors."

"So that's what they were building," said Lizzy. "I was downtown with my mom a while ago. It's right around the corner from The Burger Bear."

"Hey, I can't wait!" said Fred. "I love pizza!"

"My whole family loves pizza!" said Sister. "Especially my papa. Pizza is Papa's favorite breakfast food."

"Pizza's not breakfast food," said Lizzy.

"You better not tell my papa," said Sister with a smile. "He makes his own. He's a great twirler, too. One time he twirled one so high it stuck to the ceiling. He told my mom not to worry because her ceiling

was clean enough to eat off. She made him scrape it off. She makes him twirl outside now."

"Speaking of 'scraping off,' what's all that on the nose of the plane?" said Fred.

"Just mud," said Brother. "It's kind of soft here, and the plane nosed over."

The plane had landed at the far end of the field near the woods that stood between Ben's farm and the river. The land was low and boggy. Farmer Ben called it "bottomland." There was a gully just before the woods started. There were stunted, twisted trees and some big rocks that stuck out of the ground. The scouts had never been here before. It was kind of spooky.

"Are you going to try another flight?" said Fred.

"I was going to," said Brother. "But I've decided not to. There's just no telling where this thing's going to go. Look how far it went on a single eyedropper of gas. On a full gas tank it could have flown over the woods and into the river. It could have flown clear out of sight."

Brother cleaned up the plane as best he could. "There's got to be a better way," he said. He picked up the plane and the troop headed home.

"There is," said Fred. "It's called 'radio control.'"

"Hey, that's right," said Brother.

"Let's check out radio control with Professor Actual Factual," said Fred.

"Hmm," said Sister. "Maybe we can even get some kind of high-tech merit badge out of it."

• Chapter 5 •

The New Ralph

The opening of a Pizza Shack wouldn't have caused much of a stir in Big Bear City. Big Bear City had lots of fast-food places. But in Beartown, which was not a big city, the opening of a Pizza Shack was big news. It would have been even without airplanes pulling signs, newspaper ads, and television commercials. But with those things it was *really* big news.

There was only one fast-food place in Beartown. It was The Burger Bear. The Bear Scouts went there often. It was around the corner from where the Pizza Shack was going up.

The Bear Scouts were on their way to visit Professor Actual Factual at the Bearsonian Institution. They wanted his advice on the idea of putting radio controls into Brother's model plane. But there was so much talk about the new Pizza Shack, they decided to cut through town and check it out.

The scouts got some extra attention as they walked through town. It was because they were carrying Brother's big red and yellow model plane. But it was nothing compared to the attention the new Pizza Shack was getting.

"Wow!" said Sister. "Look at it!"

"It doesn't look much like a shack to me," said Lizzy.

"Right," said Fred. "They ought to call it the Pizza Palace."

"Ah! I'm pleased that you admire my handiwork."

Though the scouts recognized the voice, they were still surprised when they turned and saw who it was. It was Ralph Ripoff, Beartown's leading crook and swindler. It was said of Ralph not only that he would steal anything that wasn't tied down but that he was good at knots. Ralph looked sharp and snazzy, as always. The only addition to his green plaid suit, spats, and walking stick was a sign stuck in the band of his yellow straw hat. It said, "PIZZA SHACK."

"*Your* handiwork?" said Brother. "What are you doing here, and what do you have to do with Pizza Shack?"

"My card," said Ralph. He handed Brother a business card. It said:

RALPH RIPOFF
Advertising and Promotion
Dial R-I-P-O-F-F-F
(The Last "F" is for
Fantastic.)

"Does this mean you've gone straight, Ralph?" said Brother.

"If you call advertising and promotion straight," said Fred under his breath.

"Exactly. I'm proud to say that this is the new Ralph you're talking to," said Ralph. "Tried and true, straight as an arrow, honest to the core."

"Oh, yeah," said Sister. "What happened to the old Ralph?"

"The old Ralph, my dear," said Ralph, "is dead as a doornail, a thing of the past, a forgotten memory."

"Uh-huh," said Fred.

The scouts couldn't help being suspicious. After all, it was Ralph who had tricked Papa into planting the humongous pumpkin seed. And he was behind both the Giant Bat Cave scheme and the terrible talking termite swindle. But the Bear Scouts were fair-minded. They were willing to give Ralph another chance.

"What exactly do you have to do with this Pizza Shack?" said Brother.

"What do I have to *do* with it?" said Ralph. "I have everything to do with it! Ripoff Advertising is running the whole show. I'm in charge of opening this baby. And what an opening it will be. A truly *grand* opening! There'll be pennants, balloons, giveaways, fireworks, skywriters. Why, my buddy Mayor Honeypot has agreed to slice the first pizza with a golden pizza wheel!"

"It all sounds pretty exciting, Ralph," said Brother. "But you know something? I hear Pizza Shack makes pretty good pizza. Why don't you just — "

"Pretty good pizza? Humph," said Ralph. "You clearly don't know much about advertising. You sell the sizzle, not the steak — the crunch, not the carrot — the pizzazz, not the pizza. But I have things to do. Here, take one of these fliers. It tells all about the grand opening."

Ralph turned to greet some onlookers, but stopped in midturn. "Oh, scouts," he said. "Do you realize you're carrying a big red and yellow airplane?"

"Yes," said Brother with a grin. "We realize it."

The scouts headed for the Bearsonian.

• Chapter 6 •

Gotcha!

Even as the Bear Scouts were moving
through Beartown, Dr. Boffins was moving
along the same torch-lit tunnel he had
traveled earlier. Once again he was part of
a trio. Dr. Boffins led the way. Behind him
were two white-coated helpers. They were
carrying what looked like a bathtub and
which, in fact, *was* a bathtub. If the armed
guards who lined the tunnel wall thought
it unusual, they didn't show it.

Nor did the archweasel's door guards
allow themselves to show surprise. Mc-
Greed, on the other hand, showed quite a

lot of surprise. Also a lot of teeth and temper. He took one look at the bathtub.
"What is this?" he roared, jumping up and
down as if his chair had turned into a
bucking bronco. "I ordered a security system, not a bath! Call the guard! I want

Boffins in chains! I want him on bread and water!"

"Easy, chief," said Stye. "Perhaps Dr. Boffins can explain."

"I can indeed," said Dr. Boffins. "As I said earlier, a security system for Weaselworld must combine an alarm system with a capture system. Because of Weaselworld's many tunnels and entrances, an alarm system by itself will not do the job."

"Why not?" demanded McGreed.

"Because," said Boffins, "Weaselworld has so many nooks and crannies and hidey-holes that an intruder could easily hide before the guard could reach him. Therefore — "

"Get on with it," snarled McGreed.

"Therefore," continued Dr. Boffins, "a proper security system must be able to capture and hold an intruder until the guard can reach him. To do that I shall

use what I call the pumpkin principle. You
will recall how that special pumpkin seed
exploded into a pumpkin as big as a
house . . ."

"Of course I do!" said the archweasel.
"But we can't have pumpkins exploding
all over Weaselworld!"

"With respect, sir," said the doctor, "my
plan does not call for pumpkins."

"What *does* it call for?" said McGreed.

"Goo," said Boffins.

"Goo?" said McGreed.

"*Radio-controlled* goo," said Boffins.
"Shall I show you?"

"Show me," said McGreed.

Dr. Boffins reached into his carryall. He
took out a small radio. He reached into the
carryall again. This time he took out a
box. It had a hinged lid. Inside was what
looked like a white bean. It was sitting on
a bit of cotton fluff.

Stye leaned in for a closer look, but Dr. Boffins held him back with a frown. Then Dr. Boffins removed the bean from the box and carefully placed it in the bathtub. Once again he reached into his carryall. This time he took out a teddy bear.

"Stand back, please!" said Boffins. Then he switched on the radio and tossed the teddy into the tub.

More quickly than it takes to tell, the white bean exploded into a huge mass of white goo. It filled the bathtub to overflowing. It was as though a dab of library paste had gone mad and filled an entire classroom.

Stye gasped. McGreed looked on in amazement.

"Where's the teddy?" said McGreed.

"Captured," said Boffins.

McGreed reached out and took a handful of the goo. "Hmm," he said, "it's sort of

a cross between bread dough and dog slob-
ber." Then he plunged his arm into the
dough. He pulled out the teddy. It was a
mess.

McGreed looked the teddy in the eye.
"Gotcha!" he said.

• Chapter 7 •

Help from the Professor

"This is a fine-looking piece of work," said Professor Actual Factual. He studied it from every angle.

"Thank you, professor," said Brother.

Praise from Actual Factual was praise indeed. The professor was not only director of the Bearsonian, he was chief of BASA, the Bear Aeronautic and Space Administration.

When the scouts reached the museum, Grizzly Gus, the professor's bear-of-all-work, directed them to the workshop. The Bear Scouts had been there before. It was a great place to visit. It was where the professor worked on his inventions.

"Excellent!" said the professor. "Did you build it from scratch?"

"Yessir. Except for the motor, of course. But we were thinking, professor, about putting in radio control, and we were wondering — "

"I have a suggestion," said the professor. "Why don't you think about putting in radio control?"

"What a good idea," said Sister.

"And," said Brother, "we were also thinking that there might be some sort of high-tech merit badge we could earn by working with radio control."

"I was thinking," said the professor, "that there might be some sort of high-tech merit badge you could earn by working with radio control."

"Now, why didn't we think of that?" said Lizzy.

That's the way it was with the professor. Sometimes his personal "sending set" worked better than his personal "receiving set." But, be that as it may, the professor sent the Bear Scouts home with a *real* sending set and a *real* receiving set, along with a book on how to build radio controls into their plane.

• Chapter 8 •

All the Pizza You Can Eat
Forever!

It wasn't easy, but the scouts managed to
rig Brother's plane for radio control. They
did the work in Papa's shop. Papa was a
big help. Though he worked mostly with
wood, he was good with all kinds of tools.
He knew a lot about electricity and batteries, too. With Papa's help they were able to
fit the radio receiver into the plane's body.

But that wasn't the hardest part. The
hardest part was hooking up the receiver
with the parts of the plane that did the
steering. They had to use very fine steel

wire to do it. Papa couldn't help with that part of the job. His fingers were too big and fat. Brother's and Fred's fingers were too big, too. But Sister's and Lizzy's weren't. Not only that, they were used to doing fine work. They made bead and wire rings and bracelets. They were also used to threading needles to sew clothes for their dolls.

Brother and Fred watched Sister and Lizzy do the work. Finally, the job was done.

"Well, Papa, what do you think of our radio-controlled plane?" said Brother.

But Papa didn't even hear Brother. He was busy reading something. Brother shrugged and turned to his fellow scouts. "Well, gang, what do *you* think?"

"I think it's slogan time," said Sister.

So the Bear Scouts picked up some leftover pieces of balsa wood and crossed them. When they shouted, "One for all and all for one!" it startled Papa.

"ONE FOR ALL AND ALL FOR ONE!"

"Huh? Wha?" he said.

"It's okay, Papa," said Sister.

"You're darned right it's okay," said Papa. "It's *better* than okay. Did you see this?"

"Sure. We brought it home," said Brother. "It's the flier for the grand opening of the new Pizza Shack."

"They're going to have balloons, giveaways, and marching bands. And best of all," said Papa, "they're going to have a twirling tournament. And just listen to the grand prize. All the pizza you can eat *forever*! And look at these toppings! Wow! I'm not going to miss that. Excuse me, scouts. I'm going to go practice my twirling!"

"And we," said Brother, "are going to go test our new radio-controlled plane."

• Chapter 9 •
A Knife in the Door!

The "new" Ralph was lost in thought as he walked along the path that led to his houseboat. He was thinking about the money he would make out of the Pizza Shack's grand opening. The new Ralph would be getting paid for his advertising work, of course. But the old Ralph had some very interesting "extras" in mind.

Five of the slickest pickpockets in Big Bear City would be coming in for the grand opening. The crowds would be huge. Ralph and his old pickpocket friends would split the loot fifty-fifty. Since Chief

Bruno and Officer Marguerite were Beartown's whole police force, there wasn't much danger of getting caught.

Eddie Silverfish was also coming in for the event. Eddie always traveled with a small bottle of silverfish in his pocket. He would order food in a crowded restaurant. When it came, he would sneak one of his little friends onto his plate. Then he would shout, "Silverfish! Silverfish!" The swindle was usually good for a nice piece of hush money from the manager.

Ralph had a happy smile on his face as he walked through the woods. Thoughts about swindles and tricks made Ralph feel warm all over. But as he looked ahead at his houseboat, he saw something that chilled him to the bone.

There was a knife stuck in his door. It was holding a note.

Ralph looked around. Things seemed too quiet. He hurried up the gangplank.

He pulled out the knife. He read the note.
It said:

The note wasn't signed. But Ralph had a
pretty good idea whom it was from. But
why was it so quiet?

He hurried into the houseboat. He saw
why. His pet parrot's beak was tied shut.
Poor Squawk! Ralph untied it as quickly
as he could.

"Weasels!" squawked Squawk. "Filthy
rotten weasels!"

Filthy rotten weasels, indeed, thought
Ralph with a shiver. He fed Squawk some
crackers to calm him down.

• Chapter 10 •

Flight Test

"Do you think it'll work?" said Sister.

"There's only one way to find out," said Brother, who had just put his third eye-dropper of gas into the gas tank.

The Bear Scouts were once again in Farmer Ben's far meadow. But instead of going right to the field, the scouts had stopped off at Scout Leader Jane's. They showed her the plane. They told her all about how they had put in radio controls. They even showed her how to work them.

"See?" said Brother. "When you pull the joystick back, the nose tilts up. In the air that would make the tail go down and the plane would climb."

"Amazing," said Jane.

Of course, the plane wasn't in the air. It was on Jane's dining room table.

"And when you push the joystick forward," continued Brother, "the nose tilts down. That makes the tail go up and the plane dives."

"Terrific!" said Jane. "I wish I could come with you for the test. But I've got tons of test papers to mark."

Besides being the scouts' troop leader, Jane was a teacher at Bear Country School. In fact, Sister and Lizzy were in her class. Jane was a good teacher, but she was a great scout leader. Even though she was a grown-up, she got just as excited about things as the scouts did.

"As for going for the High-Tech Merit Badge," said Jane, "I don't see why not. It's an advanced badge. But this radio-controlled plane of yours surely is high-tech. Where does the power come from? I don't see anything plugged into the wall."

"Batteries," explained Fred. "There's a big one in the control box and a small one in the plane."

Jane waggled the joystick. "How do you make it turn?" she said.

"I think we'd better leave that to another time," said Brother. "The battery in the plane is small and weak. We don't want to use it up."

"It's not a problem when it's flying," said Sister. "There's a thing in the motor that puts power back in the battery."

"It's the same with your car," said Lizzy.

Scout Leader Jane looked down at Sister and Lizzy. She didn't say so, but she was proud of their interest in high-tech things. When she was a cub, girls didn't know anything about airplanes, cars, and batteries. Jane was pleased that it was

different now. She got a far-off look in her eye.

"Okay, scouts. I've got things to do, and so do you," she said as she let them out the door.

"Did you see that far-off look in Jane's eye?" said Sister.

"Yes," said Lizzy. "What do you suppose that was about?"

"Search me," said Brother. "It's not always easy to understand grown-ups."

The Bear Scouts were all set for the test. The gas tank was full. Brother was about to turn the propeller to start the engine. The plan was for the scouts to take turns handling the controls. Fred would start. Sister would be next. Then Lizzy. Brother would take over for the landing, which was the trickiest part.

The motor caught on the first turn of the propeller. The plane snarled up into the air, as it had earlier. But this time it was under control — radio control.

"Okay, Fred," said Brother. "Put her in a slow climb."

Fred pulled back on the stick just a little. The plane climbed until it was about two hundred feet in the air. It was a beautiful sight!

"Wow!" said Sister.

"Wowee!" said Lizzy.

"Okay," said Brother. "Put her into a slow turn."

Fred moved the joystick a little to the left. It was amazing! The plane was doing exactly as it was told.

"Let Sister take over now," said Brother.

Sister took over and kept the plane flying in big wide circles. It was very exciting.

"May I have my turn now?" said Lizzy.

When Lizzy took over the controls, things began to go wrong — very wrong. The plane started to twist and turn. Then it veered and headed straight for the far end of the field.

"No, Lizzy! No!" cried Brother. "Keep on circling!"

"I'm trying! I'm trying!" cried Lizzy.

Brother grabbed the controls. He pushed the joystick every which way. But nothing did any good. "I don't understand!" said Brother. "It's as though some force is pulling it away from us!"

The plane was now over the gully. It went into a dive.

"It's going to crash! It's going to crash!"
cried Lizzy.

"After it!" shouted Brother as the plane
dived into the gully.

• Chapter 11 •

Down a Weasel Hole

"Careful! The sides are steep!" said Brother when they reached the edge of the gully.

"Steep and mucky," said Sister.

They looked around as they climbed down. The plane was nowhere in sight.

"It could be anywhere," said Lizzy. "Like behind one of those big rocks."

The jagged rocks stuck out of the ground like giant teeth.

"Maybe it flew into the woods," said Fred.

"I don't think so," said Brother. "I'm

pretty sure it came down right around here somewhere."

"This is a pretty spooky place," said Lizzy.

"Can't help that," said Brother. "We've got to find that plane. Come on. Let's spread out."

"Let's not and say we did," said Sister.

"Yeah," said Lizzy. "Let's stick together."

Brother led the way. He was the first one to spot the plane. It hadn't crashed at all. It had made a safe landing on a dry grassy spot. Maybe the only dry grassy spot in the gully. Brother went over and got the plane.

"Thank goodness!" he said. "It's not even damaged."

"That's a relief!" said Fred.

"Yeah," said Sister. "All that work!"

"Shhh!" said Lizzy. "I hear someone coming!"

"I don't hear anything," said Sister.

Brother knew better than to argue with Lizzy's amazing hearing. It had saved the Bear Scouts more than once. "Quick!" he said. "Behind this rock."

Lizzy was right, of course. Someone *was* coming.

"Look!" hissed Sister. "It's Ralph."

"Is it the new Ralph or the old Ralph?" said Fred.

"The way he's sneaking along, I'd say it's the old Ralph," said Brother.

"What's that he's carrying?" said Lizzy.

"It looks like a pizza box," said Brother.

"This is a funny place to be delivering pizza," said Sister.

Ralph had come out of the woods on the other side of the gully. He seemed to know exactly where he was going. He didn't slip and slide the way the scouts had. He climbed down a stone stairway. Now he was sneaking along, keeping his head down. He headed straight for the spot where the plane had landed. When he got there, he took a quick look around. Then he reached down and took hold of the grassy spot. It lifted like a lid. Beneath it was a hole. It was just big enough for Ralph and his pizza box. He lowered the lid after him.

"Are you thinking what I'm thinking?" said Brother.

"I am if you're thinking weasels," said Fred.

"No doubt about it," said Sister.

"Weasels for sure," said Lizzy.

"Come on," said Brother.

"What are we gonna do?" said Fred.

"Follow Ralph, of course," said Brother.

"Won't that be dangerous?" said Fred.

"Not as dangerous as not following him," said Brother.

"Brother's right," said Sister. "Ralph's bad enough by himself. But when he hooks up with the weasels, that's real trouble."

"What are we going to do with the airplane?" said Lizzy.

"We'll cover it with brush and hide it behind this rock," said Brother. "We'll get it when we come back."

"Don't you mean *if* we come back?" said Fred.

Working quickly, the Bear Scouts hid the plane. Then they lifted the grass lid, and down the weasel hole they went.

• Chapter 12 •

Waiting for Ralph

When McGreed heard that the security
system was ready, he was so pleased he
did a little dance. Stye had never seen the
archweasel dance before. "Are you all
right, chief?" he asked.

"I'm *better* than all right," said Mc-
Greed. He grasped Stye's wrist in a fierce
grip. McGreed was not only the smartest
and meanest weasel in Weaselworld, he
was the strongest. "Do you want to know
why?" said McGreed.

Stye was in such pain, he couldn't
speak. He shook his head yes.

"Because, my friend," said McGreed, "once this security system is in place, we can get on with the death and destruction of the Bear Scouts!" His little yellow eyes narrowed. His needle-sharp teeth showed at the corners of his cruel mouth. Just the thought of the Bear Scouts put McGreed in a fury. "Well?" he roared after a brief moment of hatred. "Are we going to have a test, or aren't we?"

The test was to take place in the tunnel just outside McGreed's office. "Sir," said Dr. Boffins when McGreed was seated. "This is our master control. As you can see, it has rows of buttons. Each button shows a security spot. This first button protects your office. When an intruder passes this spot, the button lights up. You simply press the button. One of my helpers will be our intruder." Boffins handed the master control to McGreed.

"Your helper won't be needed," said Mc-Greed with a weasely grin. "I'm expecting that fool Ralph Ripoff any minute. He will be our intruder."

McGreed stared happily into the tunnel, his finger at the ready, waiting for the light to go on.

• Chapter 13 •

In the Dough

Ralph had come this way many times. He was of two minds as he moved along the Weaselworld tunnel. One mind was just plain scared. That's the way it was dealing with the weasels. There was something about them that turned his knees to jelly. Especially that McGreed. Ralph shivered just thinking about him.

Ralph's other mind was filled with lovely thoughts of money. Those weasels may be scary. But their money was as good as gold. In fact, it *was* gold.

To keep his courage up, Ralph began to sing a little song. A song about money.

Give me that big money,
That big, big money,
Better than honey,
That big, big money,
Good for what ails ya,
Never fails ya,
Good for each and every
Single ache and pain,
Satisfies the spirit,
Nourishes the brain . . .

Ralph began to sweat. It wasn't just the warmth of the pizza box that caused it. He was getting close. One last turn and he would know his fate: big trouble or big money. Maybe even big, big money.

What a relief, then, when he rounded that last bend! The archweasel himself was waiting! And he was smiling! But what was that thing with the buttons?

"Brought you a little present, chief. Just a token of my esteem." Hmm, why was that light going on?

The next thing Ralph saw was a mountain of mushy dough. He had a very good view of it because he was *inside* it. It was exploding all around him. What was happening? What were the weasels going to do? Bake him in a pie like the four-and-twenty blackbirds?

His cry of "He-l-l-l-p!" was smothered in
the mountain of dough. It looked as
though Ralph might be smothered, too.

The Bear Scouts saw the whole thing.
They had followed Ralph down the weasel
hole. Keeping out of sight, they followed
him down the twisting stairs, down the

rickety ladders, into the very heart of Weaselworld.

"Wow!" said Fred. "Did you see that?"

"We saw it!" said Sister.

"Poor Ralph!" said Lizzy.

"What do you make of it?" said Fred.

"I don't know what to make of it," said Brother.

"Maybe it's some kind of April Fool's joke," said Lizzy.

"It's not even April," said Fred.

"It looked like some kind of test to me," said Brother.

"A test of what?" said Fred.

"It's hard to say," said Brother. "Maybe a test of some kind of secret weapon."

"A secret sci-fi weapon!" said Sister.

"Come on," said Brother. "Let's get out of here. We've got to go see Gramps."

Grizzly Gramps, who was Brother and Sister's grandfather, was the Bear Scouts' expert on the weasels.

• Chapter 14 •

Pizza Party

"Mmm," said McGreed. "Very tasty. You say it's called pizza?"

"Yum!" said Dr. Boffins.

"Ditto!" said Stye.

Ralph hadn't smothered, of course. The weasels had rescued him *and* the pizza. While Ralph was very upset about his suit — it looked as though he *had* been baked in a pie — he was glad the weasels weren't angry with him. The pizza he had brought was a big hit. McGreed, Dr. Boffins, and Stye all had seconds. Soon all that was left of the pizza was the box. In fact, the weasels were interested in the whole idea of the Pizza Shack — especially McGreed.

"Tell me more about this Pizza Shack," said McGreed, licking his fingers.

"What do you want to know, chief?" said Ralph.

"Everything," said McGreed.

So Ralph told him everything. He told him about the pennants, the balloons, the marching bands, the grand opening, the

Tell me more about this Pizza Shack.

twirling tournament. Everything! Mc-Greed was especially interested in the grand opening and the twirling contest.

"You say that everybody will be there?" said McGreed.

"Everybody who is anybody," said Ralph.

"Does that include the Bear Scouts?" said McGreed.

"They wouldn't miss it," said Ralph. "You see, Brother and Sister's dad is the favorite to win the twirling tournament."

"How about that grandfather of theirs?" said McGreed.

"As I said, chief," said Ralph, "everybody who is anybody will be there."

"Very good, Ralph," said McGreed. "You've been a big help."

"Glad to do it. Call on me at any time," said Ralph. "But — er — I'm a little short of money right now and . . ."

"Of course," said McGreed. He motioned to Stye, who tossed Ralph a small bag of money.

"But, chief," said Ralph. "Look at this suit. This will hardly pay my cleaning bill."

"Just a first payment, my friend," said McGreed. "There will be a much larger payment later in the game."

Ralph shrugged. "It's your call, chief. You know where to reach me. Well, so long, fellows."

McGreed watched as Ralph disappeared into the tunnel's gloom. "Friends," said McGreed, "that babbling fool has just given me an idea that will not only take care of the Bear Scouts but will at last help us reach our sworn goal."

"You mean, take over Bear Country lock, stock, and honeypot?" said Stye.

"Exactly," said McGreed. "Dr. Boffins, come into my office. We need to talk again."

• Chapter 15 •

"You Should Have Seen It, Gramps!"

The Bear Scouts had come straight
from Farmer Ben's far meadow to
Gramps and Gran's house. They were
in Gramps's study. They were telling
about the strange events of the day:
the plane being pulled off course, the
spooky gully, following Ralph down
the weasel hole, and finally watching
him get swallowed up by a mountain
of goo.

"Really, Gramps," said Brother. "You
should have seen it. It was like a scene

from the weirdest sci-fi horror movie
you've ever seen!"

"Yeah!" said Fred. "Like a scene from
The Creeping Unknown."

"Or *The Slime Creature from Beneath
the Bog*," said Sister.

"Or *The Revenge of the Jellied Brain*,"
said Lizzy.

"I'm afraid I've never seen any of those
movies," said Gramps. "But I do have some
questions."

"Ask us anything," said Brother.

"What made you think it was some
kind of test?" said Gramps.

"That's what it looked like," said Brother. "Ralph going down this tunnel carrying a box. The head weasel with some kind of control thing with buttons. One of 'em lights up, and WHAMMO! This white stuff grabs Ralph."

"What sort of white stuff?" said Gramps.

"It looked like some kind of mushy dough," said Brother.

"It just swallowed him up," said Fred.

"It was kind of scary," said Sister.

"Poor Ralph," said Lizzy.

"I wouldn't worry too much about Ralph," said Gramps. "The weasels might rough Ralph up a bit. But they wouldn't allow any real harm to come to him. He's too valuable to them." Gramps paused. "You said Ralph was carrying a box. What sort of box?"

"It looked like a pizza box," said Brother.

"Hmm," said Gramps. "I wonder if all this has anything to do with that Pizza Shack Ralph's mixed up with. I can't imagine what. But when Ralph and the weasels get together, anything's possible."

"Do you think it might be part of some weasel scheme to take over Bear Country?" said Sister. "You know, like with the humongous pumpkin."

"I don't see how they could do that with bread dough, even radio-controlled bread dough," said Gramps. "But I suppose anything's possible." Gramps stopped to think. "Say, are you planning to go to the Pizza Shack's grand opening?"

"Wouldn't miss it," said Brother. "My dad's entering the twirling tournament. You should see him twirl. He's got a good chance of winning."

"Here's what we'll do," said Gramps. "I'll pick you up in my truck, and we'll go together. Just to keep an eye on things."

• Chapter 16 •

A Daring Plan

If Sister and the rest of the troop had known what McGreed was planning, they *really* would have been scared. Not only had he come up with a scheme to reach his sworn goal — to steal Bear Country from the bears, to take over Bear Country lock, stock, and honeypot — he was going to use the Bear Scouts to *do* it. McGreed's plan was so daring, it scared even Stye.

"But, sir," said Stye. "Isn't that cubnapping?"

"That's what it is," said McGreed. "And if we're lucky, I'll be Grampsnapping, too.

You heard Ralph. Everybody will be there. We'll swoop down on 'em so fast they won't know what's happening — and all by radio control. Once those Bear Scouts are in our power, there'll be no stopping us. We'll just move our cannons onto the high ground, and Bear Country will be ours. The bears won't lift a finger. They'll be too worried about their precious scouts."

There was a knock at the door. "That'll be Boffins. Let him in."

"Well?" said McGreed as Dr. Boffins entered. "What is your answer? Will my plan work?"

"Here's your answer," said Dr. Boffins. He handed McGreed a large pill. "Handle it with care, sir," said Boffins. "That pill has enough helium in it to send us all sky-high."

"Helium?" said McGreed.

"It's the gas that makes lighter-than-air aircraft lighter than air," explained Boffins.

"Will it work?" said McGreed.

"I've combined the lifting power of helium with the pumpkin principle," said Dr. Boffins. "But there is one thing you must understand, sir. The pill must be mixed into the pizza dough exactly three and a half minutes before twirling."

"Stye," said McGreed. "Send for Ripoff. It's time for him to start earning his money."

• Chapter 17 •

Tops in Toppings

When the Bear Scouts finally got to the
Pizza Shack's grand opening, they couldn't
help feeling a little silly. Gramps felt the
same way. The reason they felt silly was
that the grand opening just didn't look
like some kind of weasel plot.

It was all so much fun. It was all balloons and pennants, friendly faces and
happy laughter. The restaurant itself was
a bright building with red-and-white-
striped awnings. There was a big sign
shaped like a heart that said, "FROM OUR
OVENS TO YOUR TUMMY — WITH LOVE."

There was a really tall sign. At the top it said, "PIZZA SHACK. TOPS IN TOPPINGS. SEVENTY-TWO TOPPINGS. COUNT 'EM." Sister counted them. There were seventy-two.

And everybody who was anybody *was* there: Scout Leader Jane, Fred's parents, Lizzy's parents, Mayor Honeypot (he got a big hand when he sliced the first pizza with a golden pizza wheel, but when he started to make a speech the crowd shouted, "No speech! No speech!"). Brother and Sister's parents were there. But, of course, they weren't together. Mama was with Farmer and Mrs. Ben. Papa was lined up for the twirling tournament, which was going to be the big event of the day.

Yes, everybody who was anybody was there. And there was one thing they all agreed on. It was that Ralph Ripoff had done a wonderful job of putting together the Pizza Shack's grand opening. It wasn't an easy thing to admit. Everybody there had been cheated or tricked by Ralph at one time or another. But fair was fair. There was no question about it. Ralph had done a great job. Everything had run like clockwork: the balloon release, the marching bands, the ribbon cutting. Ralph was everywhere, greeting folks, slapping backs, shaking hands.

Of course, not *everything* went smoothly. You really couldn't expect that with something as big as the Pizza

Shack's grand opening. Chief Bruno placed a couple of strangers under arrest and returned some wallets to bears who hadn't known they were missing. Officer Marguerite looked into a fuss in the restaurant and collared a fellow named Eddie Silverfish.

But the most important thing about the day — the reason for the whole grand opening — was *pizza*! And by all reports, Pizza Shack's pizza was delicious! Folks were eating pizza in the sit-down part of

the restaurant as if there were no tomor-
row. Cars were lined up at the take-out
window for blocks.

It was almost time for the twirling
tournament. The Bear Scouts and Gramps
stopped by to wish Papa luck. There was a
long line of tables. On each table was a
baking board and a flour shaker. There
was a twirler behind each table. Papa and
a couple of others were doing twirling ex-
ercises. "Way to go, Papa!" shouted Sister.
Papa smiled and made the thumbs-up
sign.

Ralph, who was in charge of the tournament, was moving along the line of tables. Behind him was a Pizza Shack
busbear pushing a cart. On the cart was a
huge pile of chunks of dough. As Ralph
walked along the line of tables, he
smacked a big chunk of dough onto each
baking board. The big event was about to
begin.

• Chapter 18 •

"Ready! Get Set! *Twirl!*"

The dough was ready. The twirlers were
ready. The crowd was ready. And what a
crowd it was! The biggest that downtown
had seen since the parade for the
Beartown baseball team the year they
were champions.

Certainly Ralph was ready. He climbed
onto a small platform. "Your attention,
please!" he said in a booming voice. "The
great Pizza Shack twirling tournament is
about to begin! We're offering fabulous
prizes. They're all posted on the bulletin
board. A few words about our rules.

Twirlers will be judged on three things: form, height of twirl, and diameter of pizza. Any pizza that is dropped or falls apart will be out of the contest. Let me introduce our judge, Chef Arturo."

Chef Arturo got a big hand. Ralph had climbed down from the platform and once again walked along the line of tables. He had a word of cheer for each twirler. But when he reached Papa, he stopped and shook Papa's hand. Then he took out his watch, gave Papa's dough a pat for luck, and moved on.

"Did you see that?" said Lizzy.

"Did I see what?" said Brother.

"Ralph put something in Papa's dough," said Lizzy. "Just after he took out his watch."

"Why would he do that?" said Sister.

"I don't know," said Lizzy. "But Gramps said because of the weasels we should

keep our eyes open, and I saw Ralph put something in Papa's pizza dough."

"Lizzy's right," said Gramps. "I saw it, too."

Ralph was back on the platform. He was still looking at his watch. The crowd was getting restless.

"What's he waiting for?" said Sister.

What he was waiting for, of course, was for exactly three and a half minutes to go by. When they finally did, he cried, "Ready! Get set! *Twirl!*"

The twirlers went to work with a fury. There was a time limit to the contest, so there was no time to lose! Papa was one of the first to get his dough flat enough to start twirling. "Go, Papa, go!" cried the scouts. It looked as if Papa's practice was paying off.

Some of the other twirlers were doing pretty well. But Papa took an early lead. It was very exciting. Except for Lizzy, the scouts were watching Papa. Lizzy kept her eyes on Ralph. He reached into his jacket pocket. He took out a cordless phone. He pulled up the aerial and began talking into the mouthpiece. Lizzy wondered whom he could be talking to and how he could hear with all the noise and excitement.

Pizza twirling is a rhythm thing, and Papa really had the rhythm. First he twirled the pizza in his hands. Then, when it felt just right, up it went, spinning, twirling. Then he caught it, still twirling. It was getting bigger all the time. Then up again. Higher, higher. Bigger, bigger. Papa looked like a sure winner. He could almost taste that first prize: all the pizza he could eat, forever.

Then something happened that those who saw it would never forget. Papa's pizza went up all right. But instead of coming down, it kept on going up. It kept going higher and higher. It kept getting bigger and bigger, until it cast a shadow over the whole downtown.

At first the crowd watched in silent horror. Then they watched with screaming horror.

But it wasn't until the gigantic spinning, twirling pizza stopped going up and started to come down that the crowd got really scared. They ran every which way,

screaming, "It's after us! It's after us!"

"I've got news for them," said Brother to Gramps and his fellow scouts. "It's not after them. It's after us. SO RUN FOR YOUR LIVES!"

• Chapter 19 •

The Battle of the Joysticks

In the twirl of a pizza, that happy, care-free, grand-opening scene had turned into a sci-fi nightmare.

"To your pickup truck, Gramps!" cried Brother. "Then head for the tree house! I think I know what this is about!"

Lucky for the scouts, Gramps's pickup truck wasn't parked too far away. But it was far enough to be scary. Because the sci-fi pizza was gaining on them.

Gramps was breathing hard by the time they reached the truck and leaped in. Gramps threw the pickup into gear, and off they roared in a cloud of dust. The only thing that kept the sci-fi pizza from swooping down and picking them up truck and all was that they were downtown. The two- and three-story downtown buildings protected them. But once they were on the open road, the monster pizza would be able to swoop down and swallow them up.

Sister, Fred, and Lizzy were in the back of the truck. Brother was in the cab with Gramps. "Faster! Faster!" screamed the scouts in the back.

Gramps, who had finally caught his breath, said, "You said you know what this is about. Well, what *is* it about?"

"Weasels," said Brother. "But turn on the radio. I want to be sure."

"The radio?" said Gramps, switching on the truck's radio. "We're about to be swallowed up by a giant pizza, and you want music!"

"Not the FM band," said Brother. "We

need AM." He switched to the AM band. It was instant static on all channels. "That static *proves* it's the weasels!" cried Brother.

"Weasels? Static? I'm confused," said Gramps. He sneaked a peek in the rearview mirror. "Hey!" he cried. "That dang thing is gaining on us!"

"It all has to do with radio control," said

Brother. "You see, FM is static-free. But AM isn't. That static proves two things: one, that thing chasing us is radio-controlled, and, two, it isn't really a pizza. It's the same gunk that grabbed Ralph."

"Hey! That's right!" said Gramps.

"Lizzy saw Ralph sneak something into Papa's pizza dough. She told me." They were out on the open road now. "Floor it, Gramps! Floor it!"

"It's already floored!" said Gramps.

The sci-fi pizza was still gaining on them.

"Any ideas?" said Gramps.

"Just one," said Brother.

The Bear family's tree house was just ahead. The radio-controlled pizza was coming on faster and lower. It was about to make its move.

"But there's no time to explain," said Brother. "Just stop in front of the tree house!"

Gramps made a panic stop in front of the tree house. Brother leaped out of the truck and raced up the front steps and into the house.

The pizza was about to attack. Its shadow was growing bigger and bigger. It was brushing the top of the tree house.

Brother rushed out the door. He was holding a black box. It was the radio control he used to fly the plane. "I'm sure they're using a control box like this one. So cross your fingers and take cover. This is going to be a battle of the joysticks!"

Gramps and the other scouts took cover under the front steps.

"If only I can find the right wavelength!" cried Brother. He turned the dial. He worked the joystick. "I think I've got it!"

The pizza slowed. The pizza hovered. And it *changed course and sped away*!

• Chapter 20 •

Follow That Pizza!

Brother kept working the joystick as he rushed down the steps. "Follow that pizza!" he cried as they all leaped back into the truck.

"I'll try," said Gramps. "But it isn't going to be easy. That thing flies as the crow flies."

"I'm controlling it, Gramps," said Brother. "So it's flying where I tell it to. And I'm sending it back where it came from — to the weasels! Head for Farmer Ben's far meadow!"

"I can't cut across Ben's farm," said
Gramps.

"You have to," said Brother. "Ben'll understand."

"I certainly hope so," said Gramps.
"Well, here goes! Hold on tight, you scouts
in the back!"

The old pickup bucked and reared
across field after field. Gramps found an
open gate into the far meadow. Now the
pizza was beginning to buck and rear.

"What's happening?" cried Gramps.

"The weasels are fighting me! They're
trying to regain control! Okay. Ready,
now," cried Brother. "I'm going to crash it
into the gully!"

He pushed the joystick as far forward
as it would go. The pizza fell from sight.

Gramps pulled to a stop. Gramps and
the scouts ran to the edge of the gully. The
gigantic pizza had indeed crashed. It was
in a thousand pieces. There was pizza

gunk everywhere: on the
ground, in the trees, on the rocks.

It was clear what must have happened.
When the weasels saw that their weapon
had been turned against them, they pan-
icked. They turned and ran. They left a
trail of gear behind them. It led to the
open entrance of Weaselworld. There was
a radio control box. So it *had* been a battle

of joysticks. There was a book marked "Top Secret!" Inside it was a diagram of Weaselworld's new security system. There were weasel hats, weasel daggers, bits of weasel clothing.

Gramps and the scouts followed the trail down into the weasel hole. It was dark inside. But when their eyes got used to the dark, they saw something that shocked them to their bones.

It was a cage. A Hansel-and-Gretel–type cage. It was hanging from the roof of the cave. It had a sign on it. The sign said, "FUTURE HOME OF THE BEAR SCOUTS."

Talk about scary! Talk about a close call!

"Look!" said Lizzy. "There's a phone just like the one Ralph had."

"Ralph? Phone?" said Brother. "What are you talking about?"

"I'm talking about the phone Ralph had back at the Pizza Shack," said Lizzy. "He was talking into it when the pizza attacked!"

Brother popped himself on the head with the heel of his hand. "So *that's* how they did it!" he cried.

"Did what?" said Gramps.

"Tracked us to the tree house," said Brother. "The weasels were controlling the pizza. But they were way over here. How did they know where to steer it?"

"How did they?" said Sister.

"*Ralph told them on the phone!* He could see our every move!" said Brother.

"That filthy, rotten, no-good rat," said Sister.

"Hey, look at this," said Fred. He had found another piece of weasel gear. Brother recognized it. It was the thing McGreed was holding when he zapped Ralph.

"What a find!" said Brother. "It's the master control to the whole weasel security system."

"What are all those buttons?" said Lizzy.

"Unless I miss my guess," said Brother, "each button controls a gunkspot somewhere in Weaselworld."

"Good grief," said Fred. "There must be fifty of them."

"Hold everything!" said Lizzy. "Someone's coming!"

Brother rushed to the entrance and looked out. "It's Ralph," said Brother. "And he's headed this way."

Ralph was singing his money song:

Give me that big money,
That big, big, money,
Better than honey,
That big, big, money . . .

"Why, that filthy, rotten, no-good traitor!" said Gramps, bunching up his fists.

"No, Gramps," said Brother. "I've got a better idea. Come on, let's hide in the shadows."

Gramps and the Bear Scouts stayed hidden until Ralph was out of sight.

"Okay," said Gramps. "What's this better idea of yours?"

"Simply this," said Brother. He held up the master control to the weasels' security system. "In about five seconds I'm going to explode the whole Weaselworld security system."

Then he slid his finger along the rows of buttons the way you do the keys of a piano.

"Do you hear anything, Lizzy?" said
Brother.

Lizzy listened hard. "Yes," she said,
with a small smile. "Screams."

A few days later the scouts got a call to
stop by at Scout Leader Jane's. What was
it that Jane wanted to see them about?
they wanted to know.

"About your High-Tech Merit Badge,"
she said. "You earned it, and here it is."

The Bear Scouts had completely forgotten about the High-Tech Merit Badge.

No wonder!

• About the Authors •

Stan and Jan Berenstain have been writing and illustrating books about bears for more than thirty years. Their very first book about the Bear Scout characters was published in 1967. Through the years the Bear Scouts have done their best to defend the weak, catch the crooked, joust against the unjust, and rally against rottenness of all kinds. In fact, the scouts have done such a great job of living up to the Bear Scout Oath, the authors say, that "they deserve a series of their own."

Stan and Jan Berenstain live in Bucks County, Pennsylvania. They have two sons, Michael and Leo, and four grand-children. Michael is an artist, and Leo is a writer. Michael did the pictures in this book.

Don't Miss

THE Berenstain BEAR SCOUTS

Ghost versus Ghost

"You can't be serious!" said Ralph.

"I assure you, sir, we're quite serious," said the professor. "I'm going to do some research, and the scouts are going to try for the Wilderness Survival Merit Badge."

"Don't do it!" said Ralph. "Don't even *think* about it!"

"Why ever not?" said Actual Factual.

"Because," said Ralph, "Great Grizzly Forest is *haunted*. It's safe enough by day. But at night all manner of ghosts, spooks, and freaks race through the forest screaming and wailing. And not just plain vanilla ghosts. There are free-floating heads, grasping hands, glowing eyeballs!"

The scouts couldn't tell whether Ralph was serious or not. He did have a teasing twinkle in his eye. But that didn't prove anything. Ralph always had that twinkle in his eye.

"Survival Merit Badge, huh?" said Ralph with a chuckle. "You won't survive in that forest a single night. You'll come screaming out of there by nightfall. *If you're lucky!*"

"Oh yeah?" said Fred.

"Wanna bet?" said Brother.

"There's no such thing as ghosts!" said Lizzy.

"Th-th-that's right," said Sister. "You c-c-can't scare us."

THE Berenstain BEAR® SCOUTS

by Stan & Jan Berenstain

Don't miss the Berenstain Bear Scouts' other exciting adventures!

$2.99 each

Join Scouts Brother, Sister, Fred, and Lizzy as they defend the weak, catch the crooked, joust against the unjust, and rally against rottenness of all kinds!

- ☐ BBF60384-1 ..... The Berenstain Bear Scouts and the Coughing Catfish
- ☐ BBF60380-9 ..... The Berenstain Bear Scouts and the Humongous Pumpkin
- ☐ BBF60385-X ..... The Berenstain Bear Scouts and the Sci-Fi Pizza
- ☐ BBF60383-3 ..... The Berenstain Bear Scouts and the Terrible Talking Termite
- ☐ BBF60986-8 ..... The Berenstain Bear Scouts Ghost Versus Ghost
- ☐ BBF60379-5 ..... The Berenstain Bear Scouts In Giant Bat Cave
- ☐ BBF60381-7 ..... The Berenstain Bear Scouts Meet Bigpaw
- ☐ BBF60382-5 ..... The Berenstain Bear Scouts Save That Backscratcher

© 1995 Berenstain Enterprises, Inc.

Available wherever you buy books or use this order form.

- -

Send orders to:

Scholastic Inc., P.O. Box 7502, 2931 East McCarty Street, Jefferson City, MO 65102-7502

Please send me the books I have checked above. I am enclosing $_____ (please add $2.00 to cover shipping and handling). Send check or money order — no cash or C.O.D.s please.

Name_____Birthdate____/____/____

                                                                          M   D   Y

Address_____

City_____State_____Zip_____